Peppa Pig™

Peppa and the Flying Vet

Peppa has brought Goldie the fish
to the vet for a check-up.
"You've got a healthy fish, Peppa,"
says Doctor Hamster.
"Thank you!" says Peppa.

Suddenly, Doctor Hamster's telephone rings.

Brrring!
Brrring!

It is Mr Elephant.
"Hello, Doctor Hamster," he says. "We've found a
sick lizard in the mountains."
"It's a gecko, not a lizard," adds Edmond Elephant.
"I'll be right there!" cries Doctor Hamster.

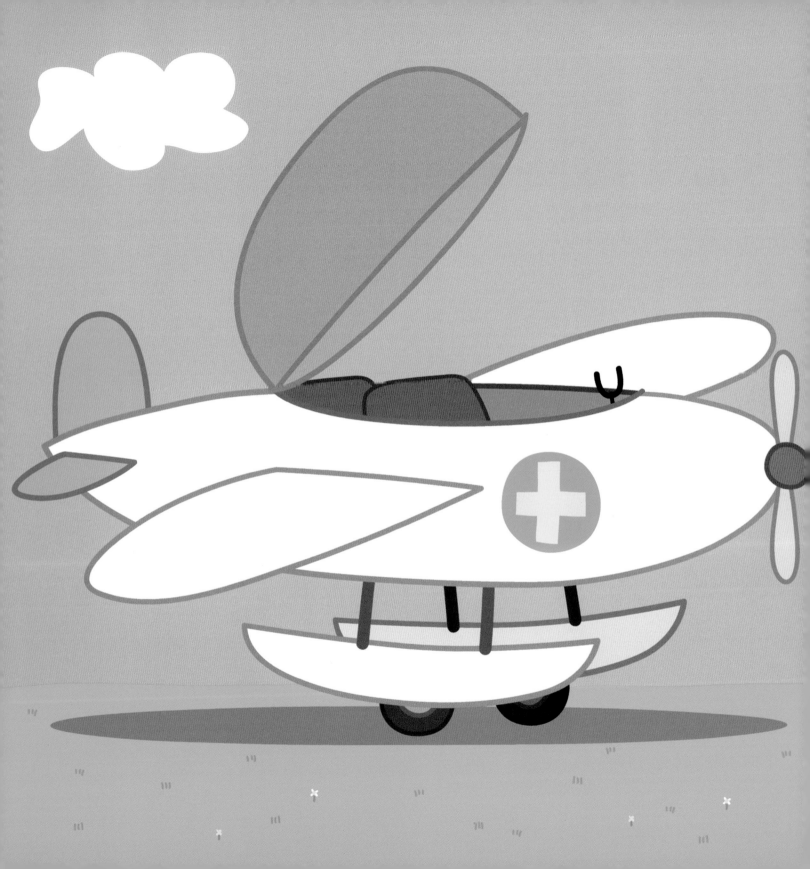

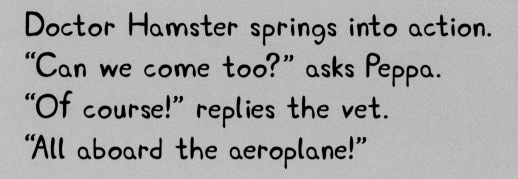

Doctor Hamster springs into action.
"Can we come too?" asks Peppa.
"Of course!" replies the vet.
"All aboard the aeroplane!"

"I didn't know you had an aeroplane,
Doctor Hamster!" says Mummy Pig.
"Oh *yes*," replies Doctor Hamster, proudly.
"I'm the flying vet!"
Mr Elephant spots the aeroplane in the sky.
"Thank goodness!" he exclaims. "The vet is here!"

When Doctor Hamster lands, she calls, "Where's the sick lizard?"

"Here!" replies Mr Elephant.

"This poor lizard is upside down," says Doctor Hamster, flipping it over. "There, he's all better!"

Then Doctor Hamster's mobile phone rings. "This must be another emergency!" she says, answering the call.

Eugh!

"Hello, Grandpa Pig here," says Grandpa Pig.
"It's Polly — she's sick."
"I'll be right there," promises Doctor Hamster.
So Peppa, George and Mummy Pig jump back into the aeroplane.

"Look, Polly! It's the flying vet!" cries Grandpa Pig when he sees the aeroplane.

"We're going into the sea,"
cries Peppa.
"This is a seaplane, Peppa,"
says Doctor Hamster.
"We can land on the water!"

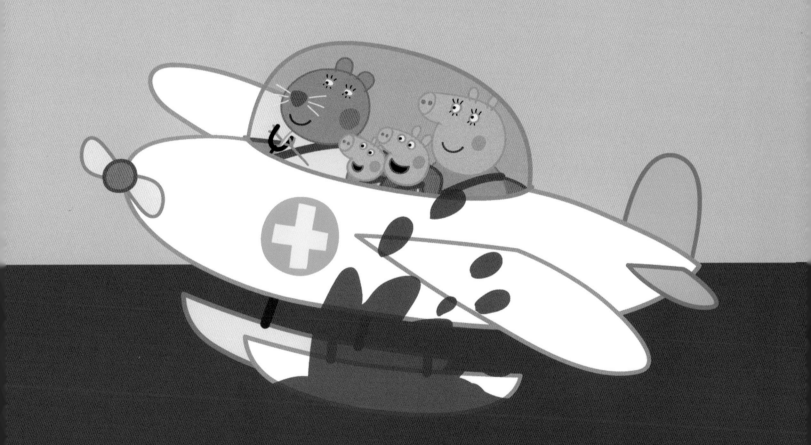

"Polly has been ill since
we got onboard," explains
Grandpa Pig.
"She must be seasick," says
Doctor Hamster.

And when Grandpa Pig puts Polly on dry land she soon feels much better.

Doctor Hamster's mobile phone rings again. It is Daddy Pig in his office. "There are some ducklings stuck on our roof!" says Daddy Pig.

Arr!

"You're just in time," says Daddy Pig.
"Mrs Duck laid her eggs on our roof," says Mrs Cat.
"And they hatched!" adds Mr Rabbit. "But the ducklings don't know the way to the pond."

Quack! Quack!

"Who can make a quacking noise?" asks Doctor Hamster.
"Quack, quack!" says Peppa, and the ducklings follow her
back to their pond.

Quack!

Quack!

Doctor Hamster's phone rings for a *fourth* time.
"Is it another emergency?" asks Peppa, hopefully.

"Yes, that was Mr Hamster," says Doctor Hamster.
"I'm late for tea! Must fly!"
"Thanks for your help!" everyone cries,
waving her off in her aeroplane.
"No problem!" Doctor Hamster calls.
"It's all in a day's work for the flying vet!"